It was the night before Halloween when Vladimir
called one last Fright Club meeting to go over
OPERATION KIDDY SCARE.

Vladimir got back to business.

said Virginia.

said Sandy.

said Fran.

Vladimir just shook his head.

Vladimir tried to refocus.

The monsters definitely had some scary moves,
but not in the way Vladimir had hoped.

BAM! BAM! BAM!

went the door.

But the critters did NOT go away.

Turns out, not only monsters make ghoulish faces,

scary moves,

and chilling sounds.

So when Halloween arrived, Fright Club was ready.

Vladimir was sure that Operation Kiddy
Scare wouldn't be just good . . .